CORGIVILLE FAIR

CORGIVILLE FAIR

BY
TASHA TUDOR

THOMAS Y. CROWELL COMPANY

NEW YORK

TASHA TUDOR lives in a lovely eighteenth-century farmhouse in
Webster, New Hampshire, a village that is not too unlike Corgiville.
Her fondness for the New England rural scene is reflected in all her illustrations,
many of which depict with loving accuracy the details of farm life as she observes them at firsthand.
Born in Connecticut, she has lived in New England all her life, except for periods of travel in England and Europe.
One of the best known and most beloved of all American illustrators,
Tasha Tudor has won many honors and awards, including the 1971 Regina Medal
for her distinguished contribution to children's literature.

Typography by Jack Jaget
Manufactured in the United States of America
L.C. Card 72—154042 ISBN 0-690-21791-9
0-690-21792-7 (LB)

1   2   3   4   5   6   7   8   9   10

To my beloved corgis

Farley, Jr., Mr. B., Missus, Megan, Caleb, Snap, Farley, and Corey

West of New Hampshire and east of Vermont there is a village. Its name is
Corgiville. It has a church, an inn, a post office, a general store, and a Civil
War statue. It is inhabited by corgis, cats, rabbits, and boggarts.

You know about cats and rabbits, but corgis and boggarts you may not know about. Corgis are small dogs the color of foxes. They have short legs and no tails. They are enchanted. You need only to see them by moonlight to realize this.

Boggarts are trolls. I believe they come from Sweden, but I'm not sure. The boggarts that live in Corgiville are the olive green kind with spots. Their hair is moss, their ears are leather, and their arms come off for convenience when going down holes. They have long tails and smoke cigars and are apt to be wild.

This story is about one of Corgiville's leading families, the Bigbee Browns, and about the Corgiville Fair, which, next to Christmas, is the most exciting event of the year.

The Browns live on a farm outside the village. There are Mr. and Mrs. Brown and three puppies—Caleb, Cora, and Katey.

Mr. Brown raises racing goats. (Corgis use goats instead of horses.) On Fair Day there is rivalry between the Browns and the Tomcat family, who come from the other side of the town.

Mr. Brown is First Selectman and Road Agent. Mrs. Brown is a good mother and sees that all is in order at home and that Mr. Brown's slippers and pipe are in their proper places when he comes in at night.

Caleb, Cora, and Katey go to school in winter. In summer they spend their time, as everyone else does in Corgiville, getting ready for the Fair.

One summer—the summer this story is about—Cora was raising gourds to display at the Fair.

Katey, who was domestic, was making a complete layette for a rag puppy.

Caleb was the busiest of all, for besides helping his father with the farm he was training his goat, Josephine, for the Grand Race. The first prize was to be one hundred silver dollars and an enormous cup, so you can see there would be a lot of competition.

Josephine was a spirited goat with a mind of her own and a voracious appetite for things that shouldn't be eaten, like cigars, pillowcases, and flower beds. In fact, greed was her greatest fault.

Every good day Caleb worked with Josephine. He groomed her and he polished her horns and hooves. And each Saturday he drove Josephine to Mert Boggart's place, The Boggs, on the Marsh.

Mert and his brothers ran a fireworks factory. They also put on a Daredevil Show with old cars for the Fair.

Mert had a way with goats, just as gypsies do with horses. He was always ready to help Caleb with Josephine. He wanted Caleb to win the Grand Race. He especially wanted to see him win the prize instead of Edgar Tomcat.

Edgar Tomcat was not popular in town. He was given to wearing loud patterned waistcoats and to singing noisily on moonlight nights. This disturbed the more respectable citizens of Corgiville, especially the Reverend Borum Barkadiddy, who had hinted about these matters in some of his sermons, but without effect.

The reason Mert felt as he did about Edgar was because of an incident that had occurred at Town Meeting last March. Edgar had tied Mert's tail to a chair during a heated argument over the School Board. Nothing much had been said at the moment, but Mert was biding his time. Edgar Tomcat was beginning to have regrets, especially since he had heard of Caleb's Saturday visits to The Boggs.

The summer wore away as it does in Corgiville, with a pleasant round of happenings. September came in with the smell of grapes along the roadsides and a touch of frost in the air. It was nearly time for the Fair.

The village hummed with activity. Last touches were put on prized quilts. The best preserves and jellies were selected from the summer's labors. The largest and most perfect vegetables were carefully harvested.

The ladies of the Corgiville Congregational Church put on a splendid supper and held a meeting to complete plans for their float at the Fair.

Each day the sound of hammers could be heard as booths were put up and the grandstand strengthened. Mert's fireworks factory was going full blast. Everyone in Corgiville was doing something for the Fair.

Caleb felt a keen excitement. He was confident about Josephine and her potential for speed. He spent more time than ever over her appearance and her diet. He watched her weight like a teenager.

Josephine was in perfect condition—but she was hungry.

Mr. Brown commended Caleb for his perseverance. Mrs. Brown thought anxious and motherly thoughts about her son and the race.

Mert Boggart suggested that Caleb put a padlock on Josephine's stable door at night. He didn't like the "lay of the land" over at Edgar's. "You never know what might happen," he cautioned, "especially at the Fair. Don't leave her unguarded, not for a moment!"

Meantime, on the other side of town, Edgar Tomcat was busy with his billy goat, Red Pepper. He bragged all over Corgiville about Red Pepper's superior qualities.

Mrs. Horatio Rabbit said she had heard that someone else had heard, from a friend's cousin's sister, that Edgar Tomcat was betting on the race.

"Making bets with money! How shocking!"

It was the day before the Fair, and the exhibits were arriving. The tents were up, and already there was a smell of fried potatoes and hotdogs mixed with the brisk autumn air and the scent of asters.

Everyone was excited, but Caleb was the most excited of all. He felt sure Josephine could win, but would she? The suspense was tantalizing.

At last it was the day of the Fair. Mr. Bigbee Brown and the town fathers gave
speeches.

They fired off the cannon that stood in front of the Civil War statue. Everyone
cheered and waved flags, the Corgiville band struck up a spirited tune, and the Fair
was officially opened.

There was the Big Tent, where vegetables, fruit, preserves, flowers, and fancywork
were shown. There was the Poultry Shed, the Goat and Guinea Pig Barns, the
Ginger-Beer Stand, the Peep Show, and the Merry-Go-Round, with a calliope and

dashing wooden goats with flowing beards. There were runaway pigs and lost puppies, and tabby cats selling cotton candy. There were boggarts with patent-medicine remedies and old corgis with trained fleas. IT WAS WONDERFUL!

Caleb found it hard not to leave Josephine and visit the tempting exhibits. However, he remembered Mert's words of warning and remained faithfully by her stable door. He wondered what the rest of the family were doing. No doubt Father would be looking at farm machinery or "talking cattle." Mother was probably comparing cakes and pies with Mrs. Rabbit and the church ladies.

Katey would surely be with the Sunday School group in the fancywork section.

Cora should be with her gourd exhibit, but she wouldn't be; she would be at the ice-cream stall or the cotton-candy stand.

And what would Mert be doing? Probably setting up the fireworks or working with the Daredevils.

It was hard waiting, especially when lunch time came round. Caleb saw everyone
going into the lunch tents. He smelled good things like baked beans and apple pie.
He had eaten his own lunch before ten o'clock, and now he felt painfully hollow
inside.

At this very moment who should saunter by but Edgar Tomcat, with some delicious-
looking hotdogs in a basket.

Edgar stopped and admired Josephine. Caleb was flattered.

"I'm afraid you're going to give me some keen competition!" said Edgar.

"That's what I aim to do, sir," replied Caleb modestly.

Edgar purred pleasantly. "You look hungry. Would you like a hotdog?"

Caleb's mouth fairly watered. Edgar's feelings might be hurt if he refused, and besides, Edgar was being so sporting about Josephine. Caleb took a hotdog.

Edgar continued to talk in a flattering sort of "man to man" tone, and Caleb felt pleased and important. But he felt sleepy, and he rather wished Edgar would go away.

In fact, he felt dizzy, and Edgar's purring sounded like a motor in his ears. Or *was* it a motor? Caleb really didn't know, for he had fallen sound asleep in the straw. The hotdog had contained a soporific powder!

Edgar switched his tail maliciously and left, only to reappear a moment later with a box containing thirteen heavy mince pies and twenty-two strong five-cent cigars.

While Caleb slept, Edgar fed all these things to greedy Josephine, who gobbled them up with pleasure. She was tired of diets.

She got rounder and rounder, and at the nineteenth cigar (she had already eaten the pies) she collapsed, groaning.

Edgar Tomcat now left this deplorable scene, purring loudly, and feeling very much pleased with himself. Already he seemed to feel the jingle of one hundred silver dollars in his pocket. It was half an hour before race time!

The bell rang for saddling and bridling. Still Caleb slept and Josephine groaned. It was fifteen minutes before race time!

The Browns were in the grandstand, watching and waiting.
It was ten minutes before race time!
Caleb woke up.

Merton Boggart was checking his rockets before leaving for the race when Caleb reached him, barking out the awful tale of what had happened.

Boggarts are resourceful. Mert saw instantly that there was but one thing to do. Grabbing an armful of rockets, he jumped into his tin lizzie with Caleb behind him and roared to the goat stables.

It was five minutes before race time.

They got Josephine to her feet. Then, while Caleb saddled and bridled her, Mert ripped open the rockets with lightning speed and fed her as many as she would eat. The results were spectacular! Caleb barely had time to leap to the saddle when, with a fiery snort, Josephine tore out of the stable and toward the race gate. She arrived just in the nick of time.

Bang! went the starting gun. They were off!

The spectators cheered. Dust flew. The sodapop boggart dropped his basket, and all
the pop exploded. Edgar Tomcat gnashed his teeth as Josephine passed Red Pepper
in a cloud of dust and flying pebbles. Caleb clung on for his very life. Mert
twirled his tail and gave off sparks.

The cheers turned to shouts, the shouts to yells. The grandstand shook with stamp-
ing paws.
Josephine passed the finish line five goat-lengths ahead, breaking all previous records
in the memory of Corgiville's oldest inhabitant.

The band broke into "Hail, the Conquering Hero Comes" as Caleb and Josephine were led to the platform to receive the enormous cup piled high with one hundred newly minted silver dollars.

A wreath of roses was placed around Josephine's neck (yes, she managed to eat some), and two handsome satin rosettes were attached to her horns (these she ate later). It was a great day for the Browns.

The gun was fired again, and the spectators sat back in their seats. It was now time for the grand parade, which Caleb and Josephine proudly headed. They were followed by Miss Corgiville of the Year, holding the trophy they had won.

Turn the page and you'll see how it looked.

After the parade Josephine was taken to her stall, where, I'm sorry to say, she fin-
ished off her wreath and the two rosettes, wire included.

As for Caleb and his family, they and all of Corgiville had a marvelous time.

They thrilled to Mert's Daredevils, who had never put on a more hair-raising show.
(Numbers of rabbits fainted.)

They did up the Pie-Eating Contest, the Turkey Shoot, and the Midway.

They had a big square dance at which Miss Corgiville led off the Virginia Reel with Caleb, much to his embarrassment and pleasure.

Evening found everyone hungry again, so they ate supper and waited until it was dark enough for the grand finale, Mert's fireworks.

Such fireworks! They were the brightest and noisiest and most dangerous—all the kinds one never sees any more. The rocket display seemed a bit short, but only Mert and Caleb knew why.

The biggest bang came last with a shower of red, white, and blue stars. In their

midst was a twenty-foot American flag done in Catherine wheels and supercharged torpedoes.

Then the band played "Good Night, Ladies," and everyone went home feeling there was just nothing, absolutely nothing, so glorious as the Corgiville Fair.

In case you would care to know, Cora and Katey each won prizes too.
Josephine never ran another race. She couldn't. (She suffered from chronic indigestion from that time on.)
Edgar Tomcat left town, and nobody missed him.

P.S. Caleb gave Mert fifty dollars to make needed improvements in his fireworks factory. The other fifty he put in the bank towards college.